BRANDEE BUBLÉ

ILLUSTRATED BY

ELISKA LISKA

Jayde the Jaybird

SIMPLY READ BOOKS

At the edge of the forest,
In a nest in a tree,
Lived the sweetest little jaybird
You'd ever want to see!

Jayde's wings were different sizes.
One was smaller than the other,
Which made it hard to keep up
With her sisters and her brother.

She didn't let that stop her
From trying out new things.
In no time, Jayde discovered
Just how much she loved to sing.

But since no other jaybird
Had a voice quite like she did,
She didn't want to show off,
And so when she sang, she hid.

Jayde only let her best friend
Come and hear her every night,
Olivia the Hoot Owl,
Who would listen in delight.

The two friends met in secret,
And a branch became the stage.
Jayde dreamed of giving concerts,
Sold-out shows at The Bird Cage.

One night after singing,
Once her friend had said goodbye,
Jayde saw a scary shadow
Moving swiftly through the sky.

Hank the Hawk looked hungry
And was headed for Jayde's tree.
Jayde knew she wasn't fast enough
To warn her family.

Because she couldn't beat Hank,
Jayde the Jaybird had no choice.
Her wings wouldn't carry her,
So she'd have to use her voice.

Jayde woke up her family.
The entire forest too.
They listened in amazement
As she made her grand debut.

Soon every forest creature
Was staring down the hawk.
Hank knew he was outnumbered,
So he flew off with a "SQUAWK!"

As Hank the Hawk departed,
Olivia cheered, "Hooray!
You saved us with your singing.
Jayde, don't hide your voice away."

That night, the whole forest
Had heard Jayde sing her song.
They couldn't wait to hear more—

And they did before too long!

Kallie & Tiffany, thank you again, for helping me make this little bird soar!
Bruce & Sarah, I am beyond grateful for everything always! Here's to #2!
—Brandee

Published in 2015 by Simply Read Books www.simplyreadbooks.com

Library and Archives Canada Cataloguing in Publication

Buble, Brandee, author

Jayde the jaybird / written by Brandee Buble ;
illustrated by Eliska Liska.
ISBN 978-1-927018-69-9 (bound)

I. Liska, Eliska, 1981–, illustrator II. Title.

PS8603.U275J39 2015   jC813'.6   C2014-906176-5

We gratefully acknowledge for their financial support of our publishing program the
Canada Council for the Arts, the BC Arts Council, and the Government of Canada
through the Canada Book Fund (CBF).

Printed in South Korea
Book design by Naomi MacDougall

10 9 8 7 6 5 4 3 2 1

To Jayde. You amaze me every day with your creative mind, brave and pure heart and beautiful old soul! You make me prouder than you can imagine. You mean more to me than you'll ever know. I love you.
—BRANDEE

To deda Vlastik and deda Lloyd for saving my family . . . constantly!
—ELISKA